This Is Living

Ophelia Finsen

Also by Ophelia Finsen

Lovers of Old Films

Published using Lulu.com
ISBN 978-0-9559923-1-5

This Is Living

How do you want to feel today?

Contents

Part One

Part Two

PART ONE

The Chocolate Boyfriend

When Charlotte woke up and discovered that her boyfriend had transformed into chocolate overnight, the first thing she thought was: damn it.

She'd just started a strictly no chocolate diet three days ago and was determined to lose a couple of stones. Everyone knew Charlotte was a chocoholic, and she herself knew it wasn't going to be easy to kick the habit and loose the weight. Waking up and realising she was now involved with a giant, living piece of chocolate didn't make matters any easier.

There he lay in bed, his eyes closed. Pure milk chocolate. Every detail just as she remembered, except that he was all chocolate now. Every hair of fine stranded chocolate. Brown chocolate eyelashes lay against his cheek. She leant forward and listened to him breathe. Even his breathe smelt of chocolate.

She got up and locked herself in the bathroom to think. This was a really serious crisis. It needed sorting immediately. She didn't know how. Where were you supposed to turn when things like this happened? The hospital? The police? Cadburys?

She drummed her fingers in the basin. She didn't have time to go to work today. She'd have to ring in sick, then go out and try to find someone who could help. Obviously some kind of a curse had been put on her boyfriend. She'd go to the police station. They would know what to do.

She showered and dressed and went through to the kitchen. Her boyfriend was sat at the table, gazing dumbly out of the window.

"Gary," she started uncertainly. "How are you feeling this morning?"

Gary didn't say anything but he looked as though he wanted to. His lips quivered but he couldn't pull them apart. She saw the desperation in his eyes. He was as worried about this as she was, perhaps more so.

"Look, I'm going to go out and find some help today," she told him. "You just stay in the flat till I get back with help. And try to stay out of the sun."

She rang work on the walk down to the police station. Putting on a raspy voice, she told them she'd come down with a sudden nasty cold. Was on her way to the doctor's now for something to help. Hoped to be back soon. Hung up and walked into the police station.

The policeman on the front desk didn't seem to be particularly interested in her problem. He looked up at her after a couple of minutes, lowering his newspaper. "I don't see why you've come here."

"You've got to help me."

"Oh, we don't help with that kind of thing."

"But surely you must know who's responsible."

"Responsible?"

"Well, I imagine this is some kind of a curse," she said, growing particularly exasperated with the man. "Surely you people know everyone in the area who does this kind of thing?"

He shook his head, turning back to his newspaper. "We don't have much dealing with chocolate. I reckon it's the chemist you want."

The woman at the chemist really didn't understand what Charlotte was talking about. She looked at Charlotte over the top of her thick plastic-rimmed glasses like a school teacher. "Have you thought about our cocoa butter skin care range?"

Charlotte stared dumbly back at her. "Sorry?"

"Cocoa butter," the woman repeated. "It's very good for the skin."

"No, no, no. You don't seem to understand. I don't want to make him anymore chocolately."

"No?" the woman mused. "Nothing chocolately. In that case have you thought about aloe vera? It's very good for the skin."

"You just said that about cocoa butter."

"They're both very good for the skin."

"I don't think that's quite what I'm looking for."

The doctor wasn't a lot of help either. At first he thought it was Charlotte who had the problem.

"Struggling with the diet, eh?"

"No," Charlotte snapped irritably. Why was no one listening to her? "My boyfriend has turned into chocolate. It's very serious! I think he might be cursed. How do I turn him back?"

"Oh, this does sound very strange." The doctor scratched his chin. "I think I'll need to examine him. Can he come into the surgery tomorrow?"

By the afternoon she was ready to give up. She went back home to the flat, to find Gary sat in the living room. He looked really worried. There were big heavy chocolate bags under his eyes.

"Oh, Gary!" she exclaimed. "You look terrible. You should go have a lie down."

She helped him through to the bedroom. She couldn't help but notice the new texture of his arm. Smooth, like the shell of an Easter egg. An Easter rabbit. An Easter Gary. He lay his chocolate head on the pillow and closed his eyes. She kissed his forehead and felt the taste of chocolate on her lips. As she exhaled through her nose, she watched as her breath ruffled the strands of chocolate hair on his head.

Charlotte ate the bowl of carrot soup that was to be dinner during her diet. Once finished, her stomach growled. Not satisfied. Charlotte let out a long sigh. What should she do?

She picked up the phone and called Gary's mother.

"Oh, hello, Charlotte!" Andrea exclaimed. "Lovely to hear from you. Is everything all right? You sound a little tired."

"Oh," Charlotte started, wondering if his mother would blame her. Maybe it was her fault that Gary had turned into chocolate. His mother was such a good cook, always making lovely food from scratch. Gary didn't eat as well living with Charlotte. Maybe this was all connected to diet.

"It's just Gary," she started. "Does his dad ever have funny turns?"

"Funny turns? What's been going on? Has Gary been losing his temper with you?"

"Well, no, not exactly. Thing is, he's turned to chocolate." She held her breath, waiting for the lecture.

"Chocolate?" Andrea screeched into the phone.

"Yes," Charlotte whimpered.

"Chocolate? Oh my, I'd hoped that had ended with his father."

"Sorry?"

"It happens to Mike sometimes," Andrea explained. "He wakes up now and then and he's turned into chocolate. It soon goes over. Usually just a twenty-four hour thing. Don't you worry about it."

So Gary's dad had this problem too. She wondered if Gary knew about it. He had certainly never mentioned it in all the time they had been going out, living together. Poor old Mike. Hadn't he been through enough, what with having been a soldier and getting caught in that grenade attack. They'd had to amputate one of his legs. Mike didn't talk about it, but that's what Andrea had told her. Mike had lost his leg at war. Charlotte's eyes widened suddenly. At least that's what she had been told.

Later that evening Gary woke up from his nap. He could hear the base hum of the television from behind closed doors. He got up and went into the bathroom to splash a little water on his face. He looked up into the mirror and noticed that someone had shaved his head.

Charlotte was quietly watching television, feeling quite calm and settled. Her little chat with Gary's mum had really settled her nerves. She looked up from the programme as Gary entered the room. "Oh, Gary," she started. "How are you feeling? I spoke to your mum whilst you were asleep. She told me this happens to your dad now and then. Nothing to worry about."

Gary looked over at the living room clock. It was only half seven. The night was still young.

"I think I might put a DVD on after the soaps," she told him. "Anything you fancy watching?"

She looked up at him and her stomach growled. Charlotte blushed and smiled sheepishly. "Excuse me! That carrot soup isn't very filling."

Gary felt his stomach churn.

At half past eight Gary came back into the living room. He was carrying a plate, which he passed to Charlotte. There was a block of chocolate on it.

"Oh, Gary..." she started, staring hungrily at the chocolate, but feeling intensely guilty at the same time.

"You know I'm on my diet. I couldn't. Besides, it's been a few days, I've lost the taste, honestly." She looked up at him. Gary looked worried. "You don't think I'd eat you, do you?" She looked back at the chocolate. Gary scratched his shorn head. "Thank you, Gary," she said quietly. "I'm sure this will take the edge off until tomorrow."

The next morning when Charlotte woke up, it took a full minute before she could find the courage to roll over and look at her boyfriend. Relief flooded through her when she saw that he had gone back to normal. No longer a chocolate boyfriend. Thank god for that. And she hadn't been tempted to eat his leg.

She got up and went into the kitchen. Time for breakfast. Maybe a little chocolate too. Now that Gary had gone back to normal, it would be all right to have a little chocolate. Besides, she hadn't finished that bar he'd given her yesterday evening. She could just finish that up and then go back to her diet. It would only be polite.

She opened the fridge. On the top shelf there was a plate with a half-eaten turd.

Charlotte gagged and ran for the bathroom.

Who is Bridget Driscoll?

The quizmaster picked up the microphone and grinned at the sea of expectant faces. "And now for our history round," he announced. "Round four, question one: Who was Bridget Driscoll?"

All but one in the 'Herculean Hunks' shuffled on their pub stools to stare at the solitary woman at the end of the table. She returned the stares with wide-eyed surprise.

"Well, who is Bridget Driscoll?" the team captain urged his comrades for answers.

"He said 'was' not 'is'."

"What, has she stopped being anything now?"

Tony, a senior accountant built like a porkpie, started to laugh. He glanced idly over at the female team member, expecting gratuitous appreciation for his joke. The team had been formed as a strictly man-only association: delusions of extreme virility preferable. Bridget had been persuaded to join a month ago when membership rules loosened. Everyone in the office knew she read a lot, and literature was one of the group's main weaknesses. Anyway, since Jamie had moved down to London there had been a spare place begging.

"Well, come on, Bridget. Who are you?"

Bridget, having the coincidental misfortune of Driscoll as her family name, fumbled awkwardly and stared at the beer stained table. She didn't really feel like anyone. She had always been something of a mediocre wallflower. Why on earth would she come up in a pub quiz? Although they all knew the question wasn't about her personally, it was hard to imagine anyone by that name being of any noticeable importance.

"I don't know," she responded weakly.

"You don't know who you are?" Tony laughed in her face. "You'd think we'd have an advantage over everyone else on this one."

"Give it a rest, Tony," Clive scowled. "It's obviously not about Bridget. She's still alive. He said 'Who *was* Bridget Driscoll?' It's a history question."

"Oh really, Clive," Tony drawled sarcastically. He reminded her of a truculent schoolboy she had once known. He would always resort to the age-old defence of mockery to hide own incapabilities. Bridget didn't like Tony. He was one in a long line of bully boys she'd had the misfortune to know.

"Look, we need an answer."

"Question number two," the quizmaster's voice came out of the loudspeakers.

"We have to put something down." The team captain was tapping his pen irritably on the answer sheet. "Come on, people, ideas." He sounded like another one of those office efficiency meetings.

"Oh, just put down 'our team mate'," Tony grumbled. "She's the only Bridget Driscoll I know."

Bridget flopped down onto her bed and closed her eyes. Her face was still pink from the shame. She ought not to be embarrassed; the Bridget Driscoll in the question had died over a hundred years ago. Yet time had not quite removed the stigma of a vague connection. Great waves of rowdy laughter had swelled up from her table when the quizmaster had explained who she was. They had teased her for the rest of the evening until she had decided it was quite enough for one Friday evening and gone home.

Bridget Driscoll, the subject of the pub quiz had died in 1896. Her claim to fame was to be the first pedestrian in the UK to be killed by a motor car. The car had been going at four miles an hour. The guys had thought this was hysterical. Everyone knew Bridget couldn't drive (thankfully they didn't know how many times she had attempted her driving test) and she had a reputation for having her head in the clouds. It all seemed very fitting.

Bridget opened her eyes and scowled at the ceiling. At least *Mrs* Bridget Driscoll had the convenience of being dead before any embarrassment was connected to the name. Such a fate was to be handed down through the generations to future namesakes.

She was the focal point of office jokes the following week. Her fellow teammates were thorough and within the first half-hour everyone in the office had been informed of Friday's discovery. It was commonly agreed as an amusing notion that the little office blonde was capable of being hit by a car going four miles an hour. No one seemed to be able to distinguish her as a separate person. Maybe she wasn't such a thing to the office dynamics.

Someone emailed the green cross code to her work email address. Tony had a good laugh at her expense on Tuesday morning when she staggered into through the door, bedraggled from the run through the thrashing rain from the bus stop to the office.

"Still in a huff, Bridget?" he called over to her, leaning so far back in his computer chair that the back rest spine creaked in agony. "You ought to marry our Jim. Then you'd be someone every woman in Britain would want to be."

Meaning she wasn't now. That got a few guarded laughs behind computer terminals.

She glanced over at Jim Jones, a confirmed bachelor from Ireland who enjoyed trainspotting more than the thought of a woman's company for a weekend. For a moment her fantasy was released and she wondered what it would be like to be married to Jim. The life of a depressingly real, dull and unfulfilled Bridget Jones.

The jokes did wear off eventually. People remembered that it was just Bridget they were talking about, and by Friday morning another personal disaster rolled onto the chopping board. Bridget had been demoted to old news. The natural order of the office was reinstated. Bridget was ignored at her corner desk, wooden flowers lined up behind the keyboard, the computer screen flickering apathetically. The office was very quiet; most of the staff had been called to a quarterly meeting. Bridget was never invited, she was virtually bottom of the heap and not important enough to warrant an opinion. She could not complain, she had only been working here a year and she was still only twenty-six. Plenty of time for promotion, the interview panel had told her, whilst leering down at her legs.

Google was on screen and after a week of wishing she had been christened anything but Bridget, she couldn't resist anymore. She was just one of a hundred thousand people killing a few minutes, but how many had prior knowledge of the results? Who else shares my name? A writer of medieval romance stories? A trapeze artist from Mongolia? A biochemist? Bridget typed in her name.

That the woman hit by the car would have come up was a ready conclusion, but she was surprised to see that she was essentially the only person featured in the lists of website hits. There was some mention of a sportswoman, but apart from that, there were seemingly hundreds of pages referencing back to that infamous woman who most probably had been considered unimportant and unmentioned until after her death.

Mrs Bridget Driscoll had been 44 years old when she had died – already a big age different between them. Bridget had lived and died in London – a long way from Bridget's home ground of York. Two completely different people. How dare Tony humiliate her like this?

Mrs Bridget Driscoll had been hit by the car on the seventeenth of August in 1896. She had been going to a folk dancing display (Bridget hated folk dancing) with her daughter and had been crossing the road when a demonstration car had hit her. She had died of the subsequent head injuries. The car had been travelling at four miles an hour. Surely that wasn't fast enough to do any damage. Frightening reminders of our mortality; how little it takes to kill a person. Four miles an hour. What had the woman thought when she had seen the car? Why hadn't she run out of the way? Or even strolled? Maybe she hadn't seen it. The coroner on the case was quoted as saying that he hoped that "such a thing would never happen again". How things had progressed. Had he lived another hundred years modern statistics probably would have given him an alcohol addiction to numb the memory of the 'good old days' when people were occasionally knocked down by crawling vehicles.

She found a photograph of the infamous Bridget on one of the sites. A formal, unsmiling Victorian family portrait, awkward and starched, smiles too hard to hold.

There was Bridget, in her black dress; dark hair scraped back, a neat center parting. Hands held in her lap and a white ring drawn around her head to point out that this definitely was *Mrs.* Bridget Driscoll. They didn't look a thing like one another. Yet she couldn't stop thinking about the woman.

"Mum, I have to ask you something."

It was one of those telephone conversations. Inane chatter about gardening and an aunt she could barely recall who was emigrating to somewhere warmer. Britain is going to the dogs, don't you know. Although she was mad to give up such a nice house. Bridget couldn't stand it anymore.

"What is it?"

"Why did you call me Bridget?"

There was a long pause on the line. "Why not?"

"Yes, but why Bridget? Why did you choose that name? Was it your favourite name?"

"Well, not exactly," her mother answered, choosing her words with guarded exactness. "Although I don't dislike the name Bridget. It was just that having married Frank, I could hardly pass up the opportunity."

"Opportunity for what?"

She could almost hear her mother smile reassuringly. "I just named you after someone. It's really not important."

Her paranoia had been well-founded. "You named me after that woman, didn't you? That one that got hit by a car." It wasn't just a coincidence. She had actually been christened after a historical traffic accident. It was not the positive start for a child's life that any normal parent would wish for.

"How do you know about that?"

"That's not important. I need to know why. Are we related to that woman?"

"Of course not; don't be silly. There's nothing wrong with the name Bridget. I just wanted to make sure that her name was never forgotten. Women dying because of men: they should not be forgotten."

"She was hit by a car!" Bridget screeched, as if it had only happened last week. "It was a traffic accident. She wasn't some civil rights protestor."

"It was driven by a man," her mother retorted. "Men and their cars, tearing about, knocking down whoever gets in their way without a care. They should show some more consideration."

Why did it make her feel as though her mother had made a mockery of her life? She sank down into the armchair, telephone balanced expertly between head and shoulder.

"It was going at four miles an hour."

"You don't have to be speeding to kill."

She held her head in her hands. "Is that why you married Dad?"

"What? Because his surname is Driscoll? Don't be ridiculous," her mother tittered at the idea. "If I worked like that I would have divorced him straight off and gone looking for a man called Wilding or Davison. Or better still, a man with a hyphen."

"What?" Was this a reference to her sister, Emily? Emily Driscoll, or alternatively, Emily Wilding Davison. The women's rights activist who had thrown herself under the king's horse. All in protest for getting women the vote. Emily Driscoll had escaped lightly. Without the right family name, the intent didn't have quite the same effect.

"But why would you do this?"

"Why not?" Her mother did not seem to be particularly concerned.

"Because I'm not some Victorian housewife. I'm me."

"I know that," she soothed her daughter. "It's just a name, Bridget. I could have called you what I liked. You'd still be you."

No one was working when Bridget returned from her lunch break. Paperwork was ignored on desks, people excitedly chattered, clustered groups of wide-eyed eagerness. Nothing traversed through society quite as nimbly as bad news.

One of the women looked up as she heard the door swing shut, and homed in on Bridget loitering in confusion in the background. An uninformed target to be updated.

"Bridget, have you heard?"

"Heard what?"

"Tony's just had an accident. He's down there talking with the police now."

"An accident? Is he all right?" She'd be lying if she said Tony's well being was a concern, but compassion tended to come up in the face of trauma; that and morbid gossip.

"Oh, Tony's fine," the woman brushed aside her question, obviously feeling Bridget was missing the point. "He was just driving back, had a car accident. Hit some little kid."

"Oh my god." Bridget held her hand to her mouth.

"I know. He said he was only doing forty, although that's strictly between the office and the store cupboard. Officially it was about thirty. Not that anyone's going to question us, but we don't want to get Tony in trouble."

She was numbed by the blasé attitude. Why had Tony become the priority? "What about the little kid?" she asked. "Is it going to be all right?"

"Oh, I don't know," she shrugged. "An ambulance turned up a while ago, took the kid away. You should have seen Tony when he got in to call the police. It only happened a street up from here. I've never seen him so quiet…"

Her duty done, the woman slipped back into conversation with the group. Bridget wandered across to her desk. Tony ought to have been driving no faster than thirty miles an hour. Even holding fast to the legal limit didn't mean the victim would survive. She leaned back in her chair and gazed out of the window, pondering on the news. If only it was that people were hit by cars doing four miles an hour these days.

She had a good view out onto the back alleyway behind the building from her small square of office territory. The air was damp and grey. Tony's figure appeared, hurriedly moving towards a grimy wall to prop himself up. The police must have finished their questioning. For now. Tony took a cigarette out of his jacket pocket and put it between his lips. Blimp, she thought sourly as she secretly watched. The sad thing was, it would only affect him for a couple of days, then it would all slip back to normality and he wouldn't have learned a damn thing.

It started to rain, a light drizzle suddenly bursting into a torrent. Tony ran out of view, fleeing for the back entrance. Bridget turned away from the window. It should have been her who had been hit by the car. It was she who was marked out for traffic accidents. The child, the statistic, would have an unconnected, mediocre name.

This was ridiculous. If she continued thinking this way, she would will herself into a car collision. It was just a name, a few symbols on a birth certificate that had no control over her life. Anyone could be run down, and it had precious little to do with what your deranged mother decided, postnatal at the registry office, and more to do with which idiot was on the road and whether you looked where you were going.

She pulled a large assignment from her in-tray to sober her thoughts into rationality. She would make sure the line of Bridget Driscolls continued to be as diverse as life itself. No one knew what her web site mention would eventually be. All she could say at present was that she, Bridget Driscoll extraordinaire was behind in her work; needed a new pair of work shoes; really shouldn't buy anymore second hand books until she'd read the stack by the bed; and would most definitely look both ways before crossing roads.

Just in case.

Music for a Lost Dancer

It was when she had slapped Andy's stomach, commenting on his generous padding, and Andy had said to us that he certainly wouldn't marry a woman like that, that I realised he probably would. I like to think it happened that way.

But I'm skipping ahead of myself. I should tell you about Andy.

Andy was divorced. He worked as a solicitor for the same big, impersonal law firm I did: a massive grey hulk of a building with so many departments and employees you could lose your soul in there. He had never been promoted because he never seemed interested in climbing the career ladder. A lot of people said behind his back that he would have been better as a housewife. Maybe it was true enough. Even after his wife had left him and he had moved out of the marital home, he kept a very neat house, very comfortable and well-furnished. It looked like a woman lived there. He liked to have barbecues and dinners for friends and colleagues. No matter what people said behind his back, if they were invited they came because they knew Andy was an excellent cook.

I always thought he should have been a chef. He was an odd enough character to have secured a place on television as one of these catering TV personalities. In one of my more drunker moments I told him that I imagined his place in life was with a cookery TV show, him singing out his recipes whilst playing the accordion: fast jigs to indicate frenzied mixing of ingredients, slow Irish love ballads for a cool oven bake. It was original. It could catch on. Andy told me I'd had enough to drink.

The accordion was true enough; he'd played since the age of three. A little lad in his pyjamas, a quick lesson instead of a bedtime story before bed. His father, originally from Co. Galway, had been very keen on the music of the 'old' country as he referred to it in his elderly days, sitting in an armchair and reminiscing about a place that had never really existed. He had taught his son to play hundreds of jigs and reels. He'd given Andy a battered old accordion that he said had been handed down father to son for the last hundred years. Andy confided in me once that he'd actually stolen it from a junk shop in Liverpool.

The music was something that had annoyed his first wife – one of the many things, and she did have a list, literally. She left it pinned to the fridge with a message saying she wanted a divorce. To be fair, he was quite a talented musician. But she thought the accordion a bit common and made him build a garden shed to play it in. She said it gave her migraines.

It hadn't been a happy marriage, and although I hadn't known them before they made it legal, I couldn't imagine a time when they had ever really got on. It made me wonder why on earth they were married. How they had ever managed to get that far.

Although she had made him unhappy, the situation didn't really improve afterwards either. He comfort ate. I remember sitting in his living room, and he said to me with regret how he'd lost his figure when she'd left. Really put the pounds on. I politely said nothing, looking up at the photos of Andy hosting his summer barbecues the past ten years, each picture in arching succession like a freakish development of those china ducks people put on their walls. Andy was the same well-rounded figure in each scene, and she'd only been gone two years. Standing there with a grill fork in one hand, his cheeks rosy pink and a big smile on his face. He looked like a merry cartoon pig.

And now I've told you about Andy, you're wanting to go back to the bit about the stomach slapping. It's praying on your mind, isn't it?

The aforementioned incident happened last winter - a particularly cold and harsh one. I hate the cold. I had to get up earlier every morning to scrape the ice off my car before driving to work. I drove to work with the blower blasting onto the windscreen and rebounding into my face. I arrived irritable and dry-skinned.

Eleven o'clock saw a small group of workers - myself included - hovering around the coffee peculator waiting for the brew. We were cold and stuck in the January blues, bored with work and life. I'd had such hopes when I'd been studying, but since getting out in the real world, giving up on dreams in order to take up mediocrity to pay the rent, aspirations had fizzled out. I had hoped to work with archives, but I'd ended up as a data processor. My brain turned to sludge and these days I couldn't be arsed looking anymore. Bitterness bit particularly hard in the winter.

I digress. We four were in the staff area, needing that little something to get a spark going. Shuffling with our cups, waiting for the caffeine kick-start. Alan was moaning about his wife again. He was the only one of us currently married. If we ever tried to suggest he was being unreasonable, he would tell us that we didn't understand and continue even louder on the subject of his wife's feet.

No one was really listening. There was that awkward silence surrounding Alan's rant. He didn't like to be made to feel like an embarrassment, so he was looking for someone to pick on. Andy was closest to the coffee.

"You have an idea what I'm talking about," he said, narrowing his eyes as he leaned towards Andy. "When do you think you'll be getting married again?"

Andy shrugged his shoulders. "I don't want to go through that again."

"Of course you do," Alan assured him.

I stared in horror at Alan. All he ever did was curse marriage.

"You just need to marry a different kind of woman."

It was then that she had come in. She'd stopped in the doorway, in all her red-headed glory and held her arms wide open as if she was about to bear hug all four of us at once. I should mention at this point that we had never seen her before. She was a stranger. And strange was definitely the operative word.

"There you all are!" she burst out as if we were long lost lovers.

There we were indeed, but why this should have made her day, I'll never know. She embodied the meaning of curiosity: five foot three with curly red hair, a face like a horse and tiny little eyes. In an attempt to point out she did have eyes, her eyelids were pasted with pea green eyeshadow. I make it sound garish, but with the red lipstick, it did actually work on her face somehow.

She came eagerly over to us, virtually running, arms still wide, and for a moment Will looked terrified, as if she was going beat him to the floor and start kissing him.

"Look at you," she cried to Will, "With your shiny head. That's great. And I love your knees," she added to me before looking at Alan. She faltered at this point, as if realising that Alan was a bit of a miserable old bugger. Then she leaned forward to him, patted his arm and said in a reassuring voice: "Ties are great, aren't they? Those bright colours can really help us!"

Before anyone had chance to laugh or growl at that vaguely loaded comment, she had turned very swiftly to Andy and immediately slapped his stomach. Certainly a way to beat that awkward silence. "I bet you've got no reason to worry about the cold! Nice to meet you all!" And with that, she was gone.

Stunned, we stood clutching our empty mugs and stared at the suddenly large and empty doorway she had just filled. Andy coughed. "I certainly wouldn't marry a woman like that."

It was two days later when I found out that the lunatic was actually employed by our company. She'd just started working in the accounts department. She was always cheerful, never missed a thing, Will – another accountant – had told me as he added a fifth spoonful of sugar into his coffee. I don't think he was counting anymore.

"I bought a new pair of shoes, had them on for the first time yesterday," he confided in the manner of someone who had just spent a month's housekeeping on something frivolous. "She noticed." He went on to tell me, that upon bumping into her at the water cooler, she had greeted him and said: 'Hey Will, are those new shoes? You need a nip for new!' She had nipped him too. Will said the bruise still showed, but I couldn't see anything.

Alan had walked by, seeing Will with his sleeve rolled up and me peering at his arm, and laughed unkindly. "You flexing your muscles, there, Will?"

No one escaped her attentions, regardless of which floor or department they worked on. She became a legend in her own right within a fortnight, some having kinder stories than others to recount about the mad woman with the calculator.

Kathy was her name. It was easy to form a quick impression of this presumably two-dimensional character: that she was desperate to please, far too friendly and eager for her own good, and incredibly loud. Not someone you could imagine sitting down for a quiet moment to philosophise on life.

In fact, I think she was in a lot of ways quite a private person. The KATHY Kathy we saw at work was just a side of a persona she decided to share with us. It didn't mean that was it. Most people never looked, but I like to think I noticed. Occasionally other personas filtered through.

St Valentine's Day that year had been the usual embarrassing affair. The pretty girls in the office got cards and flowers, the married men boasted about the romantic dinners they had planned for their wives that evening. I hated the day, personally. It made me feel out of synch. That year was a slight exception. Someone left two red roses attached to my car door. I took it as a joke and tossed the flowers in the back seat, although later I found out that it had been done in all seriousness.

On the day itself, the flowers barely registered as I mulled over the day's events in bed that night. The particular episode I'm thinking of saw Andy and me in the staff room kitchen drinking coffee. It was half five and we were both thinking about finishing for the day although not wanting to drive off to our empty cold homes. We were looking at a couple of boards the staff in HR had put up to encourage us to go on day courses to improve our life management skills. Build your career. Become that dynamic high flyer they all said you would be because you went to university. Not that we would have ever joined in; I think it was just better than staring at the carpet.

Two women who specialised in accident compensation wandered in to leave their cups unwashed in the sink. They were deep in conversation, laughing and glowing, and didn't notice me and Andy – the pale and the fat – loitering at the far side.

"He's so annoying. I feel like pushing him under a bus some days," one of them joked.

"Not as annoying as that woman, though," the second said.

"Oh yes," number one nodded. "Kathy."

"No, you mean, KATHY," number two squealed hysterically, mimicking Kathy's high-pitched response when she first started talking to a new person.

"I know, what's her problem? She's never out of your face."

"And with a face like that, I wish she was!"

They both laughed like witches and strolled out of the kitchen. I shared a look with Andy. "I think I'm going to head off," I told him.

"Me too."

We started for the other doorway into the seating area, not wanting to catch up to the witches' conversation in case we were next on the chopping board. Passing by the information boards, we realised that we weren't alone in the room. Kathy was at the table just behind the boards, a hardback book open on the table and a pad of A4 paper filled with hurried scrawl. Although she wasn't writing, she was just staring out of the window, her face resting on her balled up little fist.

Her sensors picked us up. A second of something closer to the three-dimensional Kathy was all we got to see. Her shield went up. "Hey, you two!" she burst out, extremely pleased to see us. "Andy and Anna," she said our names. I was always impressed by the fact that she had learned everybody's names, down to the cleaners and part time caretaker, in under a week. "Anna and Andy. Andy and Anna. Sounds like a comedy duo," she said, more to herself than us, repeating our names and tilting her head one way then the other to see if it made any difference to the sound.

"Kathy," I nodded to her, feeling that one of us should talk back. Andy just stood there dumbly, hands in pockets. "You're not staying late are you? Not got any romantic dinners to rush to?" I joked. It dawned on me then that I didn't actually know a single thing about her apart from the fact that she was called Kathy. She knew our names, our lives. She noticed when we had new shoes on for the first time or if we'd lost a little weight. She complimented us on the choice of suit we wore for work that day.

"Oh no," she said easily. "I live alone."

"Well, what do you know!" Andy suddenly laughed. "So do we!"

He made it sound as though it was a surprising revelation, to look at us. I glanced over at him, a little taken aback by his jovial comment. Andy had marked Kathy down as a hysterically crazed fiend sent to this earth to embarrass and annoy. I had seen him hide under his desk to avoid being caught by her. What he said next only shocked me further.

"Hey, why don't we three go out to dinner?"

"That's a great idea, Andy!" Kathy enthused. "I'll just go get my coat."

I was getting caught up in something that I had no control over. "Why did you just say that?" I hissed as Kathy left the staff room.

"Well, it's better than sitting home alone feeling sorry for ourselves," he defended his suggestion awkwardly, not looking me in the eye.

We'd walked out to the car park together and it was then that I'd found those two roses. Kathy said I had a secret admirer, and credit to her, she made it sound as though it was really possible. It just made me more embarrassed and I threw the flowers into the back seat to try and give myself an air of nonchalance. Frankly, my dear, I couldn't give a damn.

I never got to know Kathy as well as Andy did. During the next few months, I saw less of Andy and he saw a lot more of Kathy. She was still the same with most people: overtly enthusiastic, making certain that she took the time to say hello. As if we'd take great offence if she didn't react. But with Andy she was different. At work she would stop and talk to him for longer, and he would listen to her. It was during those conversations that people could slip by unnoticed, not necessarily be pounced upon. New clothes may not be nipped into the world.

It was obvious really, what had happened and what the inevitable would be. But because so many at the company really weren't interested in Kathy's life, and certainly didn't look for her or watched what she did, it came as such as shock, when, on Andy's annual summer barbecue, they announced their engagement.

A lot of people from work were there – many just for the food. An awkward silence settled down like a cloud of wet smoke. Kathy was silent – perhaps that was one of the biggest shocks, watching her gaze shyly up at Andy and having nothing to say. Kathy the hyperactive woman-child and Andy the accordion-playing chef. Neither was popular, and people didn't know what to say. I think that old cliché 'lost for words' actually described it best.

This wasn't what people were supposed to do upon hearing of an engagement, I was sure, so I jumped up and started clapping. The madness aside, I had noticed a change in Andy these past few months. He seemed happier in himself, happier to be himself. I couldn't actually remember him ever being in that state of existence before. It was good to see. People joined in with my applause, some more quickly than others. Alan's wife stuck a fork in his side to make him at least pretend he was pleased. Will turned to me and whispered in my ear that Andy must be mad. Will's comment lingered with me for most of the evening. If it was madness, I thought to myself, I wanted some too. It seemed to equate happiness.

People filtered away during the evening, quite a lot soon after the announcement as if not knowing where to put themselves. I on the other hand knew exactly where to put myself, having had one too many. I put myself on the garden furniture. That sounds terrible. I should clarify: I saw down on a bench. I was upright. Just.

When only a small gathering remained, Andy went into the house and fetched his accordion. Perched on one of his white plastic garden chairs, he set the instrument on his knee and pulled the bellows apart, pondering on which tune to start off with.

Kathy clapped excitedly, "Oh yes," she said, just as Will appeared in the patio doors. He looked bewildered as if he'd walked into the wrong house and seen his neighbours sacrificing their children.

"We're going to dance now!" Kathy continued, the volume on her voice rising. She made a move as if to dance with Will – which would have been amusing to watch. If only. I suppose we can dream of that comedy moment, the five foot three lunatic dancing with the gangly six foot two prematurely balding chairman of the local drumming society.

Andy started to play and Will ran, taking refuge on my garden seat. I was cackling like a witch. Kathy was tapping her foot in time with the fast paced reel. She started to clap and whoop and I have to admit I got caught up in it and was clapping along too, occasionally missing the beat but in general keeping a respectable rhythm going. That's how I remember it.

Kathy started to dance. I don't know whether dance really is the best word, but it seems to be the closest description. She was stomping her feet and jigging in no particular order, clapping her hands and shaking her head furiously as if trying to scare away a buzzing fly. And she actually sped up. Whooping, "Come on, Andy, play something faster!"

Which he did.

"Jesus," Alan groaned. He was still at the party, but looking as though he was ready to leave. He made a daring move for the patio doors and Kathy lunged for him to catch herself a dancing partner. She only just missed him, but pursued him around the table twice before he got into the building and out the front door.

I remember my sides ached from laughing. I looked over at Will to tell him to go and dance – maybe in my merry state I thought I could push him into the path of Kathy, I don't recall exactly – but he just kissed me instead.

Kathy stomped her way back to the centre of the patio – the decking bouncing under her energetic tirade. With that green dress and the red hair she looked like a leprechaun that had had one too many pints, either that or it had been nibbling on that toadstool I'm told they have a penchant for sitting on. Andy was grinning, his fingers flying across the accordion's keys.

And that was the evening, the start of our happy lives of no great dramas, achievements or exciting entrances. Just life. Just dance. Played out to a tune that no one knew the name of; but judging by Kathy's movements, she had been waiting to dance to this one all her life.

Bluffing It

The worst job I ever had was in telesales. And that's a big statement for me to make, considering the bosses from hell, dull jobs forcing hidden cupboard refuge to fill allocated hours, and some of the most cabbage-brained workmates you could look for.

I hadn't expected my life to work out quite as it has. In fact I'd been assured – as I'm sure a lot of us were – by teachers, career advisors, well-wishers and other assorted people who clearly hadn't needed to look for a job in the last fifteen years that if only we signed up for A-levels, then that degree, and studied hard that we would be guaranteed the good life. It was all for the taking: the fantastic job, a sense of purpose and meaning in life, the financial security to own a home (ha!) and do whatever the hell we wanted to once the long slog of hard work and study was over (and the late mornings, day-time television and nights out, but that's another story).

It would have been perfect, if it wasn't for the fact that they neglected to mention that there were only so many seats on the train to the good life. The world will always need its people to sell it overpriced book clubs over the phone, clean stale vomit out of nightclub ashtrays and take crap from small-minded bosses who probably were forced to set up their own businesses as no other bugger would employ them. I'm as bitter and jaded as a middle-aged man wondering where his youth and hairline went, and I haven't even hit thirty. I am the next generation coming into its own, I haven't made my mark and already the next line up of dynamic, innovative youth is snapping at my heels.

Telesales was my first job after leaving university; a statement featuring on many a CV with a touch of regret I would imagine. Out of academia, brandishing my masters in modern languages as if the world owed me a living, I moved to Sweden – it seemed like something to do at the time – and started applying for jobs. And getting nowhere. Weeks drifted by and the rent still needed paying. I applied for everything. I got lists of cleaning companies out of the telephone directory and called them all, offering my services. That route eventually led to my main source of income whilst living abroad – it was also my first post-university interview and something you could credit to nightmares. My interviewer arrived twenty minutes late - me waiting outside on the street in the December chill - unlocked the door and led me up to... his flat. Worry kicked, but either foolishly or bravely, I went in for the interview regardless. It was the strangest one I've ever been to. Unconcerned by any cleaning experience I had, he was more interested in the main differences between Swedish and English nightlife, whether I was planning on having children, oh, and by the way, are you catholic? After that he drifted off and stared out of the window in something resembling a drug-addled state. I mumbled thanks for the interview, hope there's a job for me (liar!) whilst backing to the door. I'm happy to say I never heard from him again.

After that I got the job in telesales. There was no interview as such. A group invitation was issued to come and see the premises and be talked at by some of the stars of telesales about rhetoric and technique. It was all very positive and light-hearted, but underneath you could see that shifty look, the hollow gaze where their scruples should have been, and the throbbing enlarged ego feeding off the gift of the gab. The thing about telesales is that every kind of person works there, but the ones who last are, to put it bluntly, the nasty bastards. And if you haven't got it in you to pressurise half-deaf old dears into signing up for a computer generated kickboxing channel on their digital television, then you really haven't got what it takes.

The surprising thing was that they actually offered me a job. Rather than an interview you were put on the phones for an hour, with a computer script that was so wooden it wasn't worth looking at (besides which, potential customers are uncannily inconsiderate in not following the script). It was at the end of this drop in the deep end with the sharks when they decided if you were worth a try. And they gave me a job. Let me put this into perspective. We all hate that dreaded call: "Hi, it's Ophelia calling from X to let you know about our fantastic offer open exclusively to our GOLD level customers. We want to GIVE you the opportunity to GET our product.... (mumbling something about a price)..." No one wants to talk to them, let alone buy anything. People selling things on the phone are not to be trusted. But even such dregs of society are not bottom of the social order – that place is reserved for FOREIGNERS selling things on the phone. I lose count of how many times, on passing the phone over to the poor sod I had to speak to, I heard someone grumble about this French woman wanting a word. French? Swedish kids laughing to their parents about my Finnish pronunciation of their name. You don't have to have your mouth right by the receiver for the sound to carry. Occasionally someone picked up on the fact that I was English, but I could never charm them enough with my bilingual talents to buy my crap.

Imagine five hours constantly on the phone. Having the same inane conversation again and again with people who don't want to talk to you. Wondering why that housewife is screaming down the phone at you to quit pestering her about signing up for your book club rather than just hanging up on you. Having a little stack of forms to fill out, one for every sale you make, the pile just as pristine at the end of the shift, whilst people sat around you have to get up and fetch more. Asking a voice that is clearly female if SHE is Rune Hagström (Rune is a MAN's name). It damn well wasn't Rune. How do they do it? If they have a magic formula or technique, they will not want to tell you.

Bribery and corruption is perfectly acceptable. In order to encourage us all to sell, the shift leader announced one afternoon he would buy us all a chocolate bar if everyone sold at least one television contract. With such incentives, surely we would have all managed, but there's always one person not pulling their weight. The team crowded around the shift leader's computer at the half-time break to see who had sold the most contracts. There was a hushed, embarrassed silence. "Oh my god, someone's not sold anything yet! Who the hell is that?"

Well, it didn't quite happen like that. This was Sweden, so it was more a case of: "Jävlar, det finns någon som inte har sålt något än! Vem fan är det?" I, sat in the common room, out of sight but still in hearing range, cringed and stared at my dinner. "Ophelia? Who's she?" That would be the girl in the staff room waiting for the ground to swallow her up.

Of course, the shame must be aggravated if we are to improve. We must suffer to encourage us to do our best. Agija was dispatched: a surly girl, barely sixteen with a bad attitude problem but very good sales figures. She descended into the common room to give me some tips. It was humiliating for both of us, but she made the best of a bad situation by avoiding my eye and texting her friends about her embarrassing day whilst we struggled to communicate. I asked her what she was doing to sell this television contract, and she asked me if I'd thought of mentioning the free weather prediction channel that came with the noughts and crosses package we were trying to sell. I'm sorry, did I hear that right? Tempt people to spend money on unnecessary crap by offering them a cheap and nasty weather channel that they have to give away for free? Is that the best the wonder child can offer me? I can't believe Agija ever sold a contract on that line of argument, but whatever her golden-tongued trick was, she wasn't telling me. She called one of her friends on her mobile and wandered off part way through one of my questions.

That put me in my place.

I lasted two weeks. It was after that particularly humiliating shift with a teenager advising me how I should do my job that I realised the thing to do was quit whilst I was way, way behind. I went in one morning and explained to the personnel manager that I didn't think it was working out. She wouldn't look me in the eye – fiend, you are not worthy enough for me to gaze upon – but agreed that it hadn't been going too well. I asked if they wanted me to work out the two weeks' notice we'd all signed up to, but she assured me that in my case, it really wasn't necessary.

And so ended my 'career' in sales.

Since then I've worked for six more businesses and had one voluntary job. And I still don't know what I 'want' to do. I've stopped thinking in those terms. You can only do what is available at the time. Making the best of a bad situation. The world doesn't owe anyone, me included, a living, no matter how well educated you might be. All I can think is: bugger it, I'm off travelling. I'm going to be in the same position in five years time as I was when I was fresh and idealistic out of university; I might as well take a break. And have a little more patience for those poor, suffering telesales callers who probably want to talk to you even less than you to them.

I still won't be buying any of the crap though.

- February 2007

PART TWO

The Trap

They had put us in here for sport. I suppose. I'm only guessing because I don't know who they are. But whoever they may be, I know they are cruel. The wall at the back is a black mirror. I know they're on the other side watching. Maybe laughing. Perhaps recording our actions. Maybe this is all for the benefit of science. I don't care. It's just cruel.

I was the first to wake. The other one, a girl barely past twenty took longer. She had a large bruise on her forehead. She was groggy, stupid when she did open her eyes. As if this was normal, acceptable. For five minutes she sat dumbly, then she started shouting: "Let me out of here!"

She eventually turned on me. "Why are you just sitting there?" she demanded. She clawed at the wall. It looked as though there was a door; the faint lines against the concrete, but there was no handle and nothing to levy against. "Who put us in here? We have to get out." She stepped back from the door and screamed. "Let me out of here!"

"They won't do anything," I told her.

Her shoulders sagged. "There's no one listening."

Oh, there were people listening, I thought, glancing over at the far wall. No point in distressing her with reality. It wouldn't achieve anything.

We were in a large, bare room, heavy walls, cold, stained concrete floor. The light came from the ceiling. Two lights set in holes into the ceiling, covered over by metal grills. Too high to reach up to. In the centre of the ceiling there was a skylight and bright sunshine poured through. It was day out there. Wherever out there was.

Two of the opposing corners narrowed into annexes the sizes of small lifts. Odd design, breaking the otherwise perfect rectangle. I couldn't understand why the room – I call it a room but it was more like a hall, an arena – had been built that way. Like everything else, unexplained. Just there.

The girl was in the middle of the room, staring up at the skylight. Sunlight poured down on her like a waterfall. A passageway up to another world.

"Maybe I could climb up there. Kick the glass in."

I looked doubtful.

She jumped, her hands missing the ceiling by a long stretch.

"You have climbing experience?"

She looked at me sharply, spitefully. As if to say what right do you have to criticise? You're not doing anything. Just sitting there, accepting everything that happens. Waiting for your fate. "I've done some rock climbing," she told me.

Looking around, she walked over to one of the odd narrow corner annexes. Now we were both positioned in our respective corners, across the diagonal. She ran her hand down the side of the rough wall. "It stinks here," she muttered. "But maybe I could climb up." A glance back over her shoulder. "Grab a hold of those grills over the lights, swing out to the middle."

I stared up at the ceiling, comparing her size to the distances she was hoping to cover. She looked too small.

Small but determined. Now in the annex, like waiting for the lift doors to close and carry her up to the next level. Hands pressed against one wall, she jumped up, kicking her legs back, her feet hitting the opposite side. Stretched on all fours, pressing out against the two walls, holding herself up suspended mid air. She could climb up to the top like that.

"You could try this too. You're bigger than me."

I started to tell her it was pointless when the building started to rumble. She stayed in her climbing position. Worried, she stared in my direction. As if I could reassure her. A groan crawled into the room. The wall was moving. We looked to the doorway, and indeed it was a doorway because a door a good thirty centimetres thick swung open. A black hole was revealed.

"We can get out."

I held up my hand, telling her to wait. "I can hear someone coming."

We waited. Multitudes of footsteps pattering. Breathing. Eyes appeared in the darkness. Ready to come in.

The tiger entered the arena and smelt the fear. I scrabbled back into my own annex. What were we expected to do here? Be torn to shreds? The girl let out a screech. Another tiger's face appeared behind the first. They were examining the room. Plotting.

The sound of scuffling. The girl shot up her annex to the ceiling faster than I would have thought her capable. Out of the way. The tigers entered the room. The door was swinging shut. I was no climber, looking up at my own annex and feeling utterly incapable. Shit, shit, shit. They're going to tear me to shreds.

A basic battle of nature. Survival of the fittest. What would the animals do? We all knew they were bigger and stronger than I was. Two tigers. I went into the defensive, not really thinking my actions through. Making myself big, jumping up, baring my teeth, stepping forward. I started to shout, stomp my feet, wave my arms. I was here first. This is my corner. Back off.

One of the tigers growled and swiped a paw in my direction. They didn't know what to make of me.

"What the hell are you doing?" the girl squealed, terrified. "Climb up the wall!"

Her squeals, her animal scent, brought the first tiger out of its bewildered day dream. It jogged across to her corner, and on all fours stared up at her with that blank cat expression felines have, wondering what this strange frightened creature was. In the background I was still dancing and shouting threateningly. Empty threats.

The girl had her back to the ceiling, pressed up in the highest corner. Sweat dripping off her forehead. "What's it doing?"

"How am I supposed to know?" I roared, still performing the territorial war dance, trying to convince myself this would keep me safe. Beyond snarling in my direction, the second tiger, also the smaller of the two, was making no attempt to come any closer.

The first tiger ignored me, fascinated by the girl. Now below her. Its haunches tightened. It sprang up, a mere moment, upwards, its body stretched long. A curious paw, claws out, swiping. It hit the girl heavy – the tiger could reach that far up. She gasped. Claws savagely ripping through flesh. There was a second as the world froze. The tiger was on the way back to earth. The girl looked shocked. Then everything sped up to normality. Her abdomen opened as easily as ripped tissue paper; intestines poured out in a cascade of blood. The girl's mouth was open. Drowning on air. Her limbs slackened and she dropped to the ground, crunching against the concrete floor. Legs in spasm. The tiger sat down and started to chew on her entrails.

Smelling the blood, the smaller of the two cats padded across to join in the feast. My shouting stopped for a moment as I gagged on horror. I threw up across my boundary line. A marker. The cats weren't bothered for the moment, having a meal in front of them. I looked back at the mirror. How could you fucking let this happen? No reply. I scuttled back into the recess of the corner. Absolutely terrified.

She's just a ravaged, mutilated mess now. Head, shoulder, one arm, are on the ground near to the sleeping cats. Blood splattered. Eyes still open. Shocked. Red bones, gristle dangling: it's all mixed in with the destruction, the sleeping felines. They are full for now. One of them took a casual walk to my side earlier. Curious. I jumped up screaming, ran to my boundary, a line marked by my own bodily excretions. Get back. The cat wasn't hungry enough to try and attack the unknown. It snarled and went back to its kind.

They're sleeping now. They'll eventually be hungry, dare to pass the line. Not sure if they'll live or die. But they'll live. When it comes to it, I have nothing to fight with. Weak, soft-bodied human. No teeth of any advantage. No claws. I need my tools, but I have nothing. They'll tear me to shreds and eat me. When time passes and it gets really bad, they'll attack each other. The smaller one will probably die first.

I look down at my shaking hands. Only a matter of time now. Just waiting until they get hungry enough. I look over at the black windows. Pleading with nothing. Surely I've done well enough surviving this far. I deserve to be let out, don't I?

No one answers.

Diamonds

Big pipe-smoker, you know. That's what they all say about me. Or used to say, most of them being dead now. But they all knew me. I was never one to hide in the shadows. Life is a thing to be experienced, people to meet, things to learn. Can't stop.

Yes, I do like my pipe. I have three to be precise, but it is the old one with the ebony inlay that is the most comforting to an old man like myself. I'm eighty-three now. Still alive and my worst health complain to date has been the flu. It's the tobacco and the whisky, I tell them – the young people, the doctors, the people I talk to. I'm the antichrist as far as these quit smoking campaigns are concerned, like that great Aunt Mildred everyone has who smoked forty fags a day all her life, lived to a hundred and one and was never ill. I started when I was eighteen – I did look stylish sauntering around the university grounds with the pipe (I was going through a Sherlock phase at the time). Never quit the old friend. Always been there for me.

The people I've known have fallen along the way. Old Nicholas died in a car crash with his wife a good thirty years ago. Alan, the man I took over from at the university, eventually died from alcohol abuse. They said he really hit the bottle when he lost that job. Professor Mayhew died of a stroke. Old Chutney, as we called him, fellow smoker and veteran of the rainy-day vigil at the backdoor was killed off by the old cancer a long time ago (although the poison of his choice was the cigar). In fact, when I think of it, a lot of them died of one kind of a cancer or another – now that we've cured the little things, the grim reaper's had to send in the heavy mob to finish us off. I remember Matthew, a post-grad I supervised when I was still working – bit of a shy type, was never going to get anywhere. He got testicular cancer. They chopped one of them off in the end. But the cancer came back. He never did get that thesis finished.

Disease and death: I've seen it all. Lord, I've even lost one to childbirth – and that was in the twentieth century. That does take me back. Megan. She died the year I turned forty. My little secretary at the faculty. I say 'my' but she was really there for the use of everyone. I tended to think of her as mine, in that I think she realised – slow as she could be – that I was the real academic power, the one going somewhere. She'd do anything I asked at the drop of a hat. I remember she eventually married one of the caretakers. Strange fellow he was, never said much. Perhaps he had a stutter or a confidence problem? I recall on frequent occasions speaking to him in passing and all he would give me was a dark stare. Not an intelligent word to share. But he doted on that woman. One scene of that simple devotion sticks in my memory. She was in her chair crying – women do seem to be prone to emotional outbursts for no real reason – and he was telling her not to cry, the idiot wasn't worth it. He didn't deserve such attentions. Probably one of the post-graduates, I would suspect. Megan was a young woman, not bad looking truth be told and they were always chasing her. Flirtatious comments and with a sweep of her long, dark hair, she would tell them to stop, she had work to do. I don't think she even made it to thirty at the end of the day.

But they're all dead, even that inarticulate caretaker. I'm still here, and I can tell you why. I enjoy life. I live exactly how I want to and my body's strong, it knows I still have things to do. It won't let the tobacco affect me. I live alone – which statistically is the way to a better state of mind. No one there to nag, rearrange things, tell you to change your lifestyle – change yourself. People get dependent, get depressed when they argue, realise they aren't going to get life just how they want it. And I've seen women argue. Nag people to death.

I feel I ought to point out here that I'm not gay. I can see what you're thinking. I wasn't impotent either, if that's what's going through your mind. I just never found anyone who truly loved me. I don't know whether anyone ever could love a man like me. I don't mean to sound boastful, but I just don't think the majority of people are capable of really understanding me.

I live alone and I prefer it that way. Of course, in my younger days I had my appetites, and I knew a very good little house where the girls would help me out. For a price naturally, but for professional attention, one must pay. And of course that establishment was quality – no diseases prevalent. I liked them young, slender, in short skirts and those low cut tops that seemed to defy gravity. Little slutty minxes. They knew how to get me going. Of course I wouldn't have wanted to have lived with any of them, lord, they didn't have a gram of sense between them. But that's not why one visited such houses.

However, I have digressed before I even gave myself the chance to tell you my reason for coming here today. In a conversation with a great nephew a few days ago, I was pompously informed that there had been no point to my life. I wasn't a risk taker. I didn't believe in living. That I knew a hundred thousand names but never a person and no one would miss me when I was gone. Which, as I pointed out to him, was nonsense – he ought to see the size of my address book.

There has been a point to my life – you should see the shelf of academic works I've written. And I have stories to tell. I have experienced life. I have taken risks. I know a story no one else knows. It's about those Queen Anne Diamonds.

I know you know the story. You think you know the story. We all heard about the robbery. About the price of that necklace and earring set – rubies and diamonds – even cut down to individual stones, the money tied up in those trinkets was phenomenal. I saw the reports on the news, I remember the photographs of the men responsible – they were, after all, professional criminals. The police knew who they were.

The point of my story is this: I met one of them, just after the robbery. I had been to the pub with a few colleagues to sample a couple of drams of the finest Scotland had to offer at the time, you might say, and had decided to head home. It was already dark, and as I was leaving the door, I bumped into a man. He was distracted, worried in manner but still decisively threatening – certainly not a man I would presume to argue with. I am by no means what some people might describe as macho, manly or heroic, although I am very tall. I always avoid fighting. I bumped into him, recognised him immediately, averted my eyes and hurried away. Two days later he was arrested and the necklace returned to the owner. The earrings were never recovered. He died in prison a few years after that.

It was just after that exciting episode that Megan got engaged. I remember strolling into the office and the women were crowding around to look at the ring – very drab and small compared to those diamonds, I must say.

Of course I had to know what was happening, so I went across to ask, and one of the secretaries explained. Megan held out her hand so I could see the caretaker's ring and I feigned interest.

I remember I said something like: 'how exciting for you', or 'getting married, it comes to us all in the end' (jokingly) or words to that effect. I then headed for my office and the women giggled. One said 'who would want to marry him?' and someone else: 'No one could ever love a man like him', which in fact I agree with myself although for entirely different reasons.

I was out of the reception office and in the corridor when these comments were made. I paused and looked back. I was already forgotten to the women – tittering in small groups like sparrows. Only Megan was silent. Staring at me. Expressionless. And she knew that I'd heard.

And it's that expression that still haunts me sometimes when I think of my dead friends and colleagues. All those people with their trivial loves and marriages and compromises, diseases picking away at their flesh and they're all dead now. I'm still here.

I like to sit by the window in the morning and look at my jewels. Heirlooms going nowhere, you might say, but who cares what will happen when one is dead? One must live for today. So I sit and recall that great moment, and watch the light traverse through the cold, hard rocks. Two ruby earrings; diamonds clustering round as if pulled by unseen forces. You didn't ask about that part, did you? Those missing earrings? I'd picked his pocket that night outside the pub; not quite as dull as you'd thought, now, am I? I do take risks, I have seen adventure. Don't let any of them tell you otherwise.

I don't suppose I could ever sell them. Too recognisable and I wouldn't know the first thing about the black market. I've never been able to give them to anyone either. Looking back, I've never really had a sweetheart. I managed the occasional fling that I didn't have to pay for, although those were rare and short-lived. Nothing that was ever really deep, ever had a future. It's like I was saying earlier. No one's ever really been capable of loving a man like me.

The Poem

If they hadn't walked into the second hand bookshop as a respite from the argument, all of this wouldn't have happened. She probably would have still left him, but things wouldn't have ended quite as badly as they did. From this unbalanced, swaying view, he could see everything very clearly.

She had been complaining about something – he couldn't even remember what her grievance had been. They'd gone out for a walk that November Sunday, and he'd just struck up a conversation about his poetry submissions. It had sparked something off inside her; those days it hadn't taken much to make her hysterical. People stared at them as they stormed by, strangers hating each other but too stupid or too afraid to go in different directions.

He'd been embarrassed by the attention of bystanders, and seen the second hand bookshop. Like libraries and study rooms, there was that unwritten rule of silence. He pulled her inside, and the sudden confines of the book-lined walls had quietened her. He'd retreated to look at the recent paperback editions, unaware that she was glaring at him.

Their relationship was at the end of its life. One way or another, she would leave in the next few months. He'd stood at the fiction paperbacks, scanning over authors and titles, looking for something he'd like to read for escapism. Poetry was his thing, but fiction was all right to give his brain a rest now and then. He almost chose that book at random, teasing it from the tightly-packed shelf by the top of its spine. It was only fifty pence; a real bargain.

He hadn't looked it again until a few days later. She'd gone out to the pub with some friends – to get drunk and spread nasty lies about how cruel he was. She could be a stupid cow at times. Sinking back into the easy chair, he'd picked up the book. It looked a little formulaic. A waste of time to read probably. Sighing, he flicked through the pages, watching the uniform print flash by. Then at the end where the left over blank pages should have been, a previous owner had been writing in black biro.

Surprised, he sat up, and returned to the handwriting. His girlfriend turned her nose up at second hand things, but he loved used books; imagining the history behind them. A name written on the inside cover or a personalised message scrawled on the first page. A ticket or a massage schedule shoved in as a bookmark as far as the last person had managed to get.

'I find this is the only way to get my work published.' He read the first sentence, intrigued. 'There seems little point in writing if it is never to be read, but I will never see my work in real print. So to you, dear unexpected reader, I offer this poem. Please enjoy it, be inspired.'

He read the poem; an original intention of scanning briefly over it turning into a submission of the senses. He lost track of time. For a message scrawled in the back of a second hand novel, this was a brilliant poem. One final word at the end:

'I have no copyright power and I do not wish to be known. I can't stop you, but I warn you not to use my words. I will make sure you regret it.'

Great poetry, but obviously not from a mind with any notion of one's own worth.

The door thumped open and she staggered into the hallway, drunk. Her hair was in heavy threads over her face. She stared at him as if already dead. "The great poetic genius at work," she sneered at him. "Misunderstood by every publisher in the world. Get back to your bank job."

For the rest of the night he sat and read the poem over and over, until he knew it so well, he could have penned it himself. It was hardly right or fair that such work was unknown to the world. Over the next week, in quiet drags of work he searched for the poem online. He checked at libraries. He couldn't find it anywhere. He could type it out again and again, beat perfect, into his computer. He printed out copies – for posterity he said in the beginning. The night they went to a friend's birthday dinner and she was seen kissing one of the single men in the bathroom, he went home and typed a submission letter. He put the papers in an envelope and posted them to London.

The day she announced she was leaving, he had just opened the acceptance letter from the publishers. They loved it. He was a success. He didn't really care that she was leaving. She had never supported him. She walked out. He didn't tell her about the poem.

It was printed in a collection that was pushed into the public glare under heavy publicity. All the major bookshops collected their fee and laid copies out on well-placed tables. It was there at all the festivals. Everyone wanted to know when his first book would be out. The publishers were offering a generous advance.

Maybe one day he'd be able to leave the bank.

The manuscript was ready, finished. Waiting on his desk. He was getting the train down to London for a meeting with his publishers. Later, sweet poet, later. It was very early. He was sleeping. Daylight was just coming through the window. The voice was a mere inch from his ear.

"I did warn you."

He jolted up with a start, looking wildly for the intruder, but he was alone in the flat. No one home. Staggering to the bathroom, he assured himself it had just been a waking nightmare. He brushed his teeth. He got the train. Signed the contracts. The editor looked a little uncertain flicking through the manuscript. The accountant clapped his hands, thinking of the sales from the compilation.

He came home in the dark. His ex girlfriend had pinned a note to the door informing him that she had visited. She had taken her things from the flat. They were completely separated now. Good riddance.

It was a day of elation when the parcel of hardback editions arrived. He went to the window to see the cover in daylight, check that it really was there. His name in print, on a book. He had done it. He knew he would. He sent a few copies to relations; kept a couple on display in his living room. For posterity's sake.

The book was met with a lukewarm reception. The newspaper reviews said it was bland, uninspired and particularly disappointing after *that* poem. It didn't sell well. Booksellers discretely removed it from the tables and put a single copy up on the highest shelves. It was eventually passed on to the publisher clearance shops. No one was interested.

He convinced himself it was because he was too ahead of his time. People didn't understand, they could only work on one level. Base, materialistic, simple. People like his girlfriend.

She turned up at the flat one evening with copies of his books. He'd let her in, thinking that was she crawling back. Wanting to share in his glory of publication.

"I flicked through your book," she told him off hand. "Bit boring."

She was just jealous.

"I quite liked that first poem though," she added coyly.

He gritted his teeth, curled his fingers to fists. She couldn't let alone. She only came over when the dream had faltered a little. Any chance to try and feel superior.

"Funny thing is," she continued, ever so casually, "I've read it someplace else." She paused, slowly opening her handbag and bringing out a tattered paperback book. "I thought this was mine when I moved out." She raised her eyes to meet his, the message quite clear. "I guess it must have been one of yours."

The book from the shop. The book with the poem. Petty vengeance?

"What do you want? Money?"

She laughed down at him. "I don't want anything from you. I just thought I'd let you know that I know. You always were a looser. Puffed up with your stupid superiority ideas. Your poems were always crap."

Bitch. "What do you want?"

"I've already told you. I don't want anything from you." She glanced slyly down at the book, toying with it. "I am going to show this to a few people though. Then they'll know what they really are."

"No you won't." He stood up. "Give me the book."

She snatched it away, stuffing it into her handbag. "Not bloody likely. I'm going to make good use of this."

"No you're not."

She continued to step away from him until her back was up against a wall. "They're all going to know. And you're going to be in a lot of trouble. I don't know how your ego is going to survive this."

"Give it back!" He pressed her against the wall, fighting with her arms to get at the bag. He had to get that book back. He should have destroyed it the moment he decided to publicise that poem. She was ducking and wriggling too much. She was going to get away. He had a hand around her neck to keep her in place whilst he went for the book, but she kept fighting back. He pressed harder, just enough to let her know he was serious. The book was out of the bag and they had an end each, pulling it like a cracker. He stood on her foot, pushing his knee into her inside thigh. Another tug and she released the book.

"Get lost," he said as he released her, clutching the precious book.

She slid down against the wall and dropped onto the floor. The sudden thump woke him up. There were awful bruises around her neck. Oh Christ. He dropped to his knees, terrified. He hadn't meant to do this. He had just wanted the book back. Why did she always have to be such a nasty little piece of work?

He yelped as she coughed, air wheezing up her throat. Her eyes opened slowly. She must have just fainted. Focusing on his face, her expression turned to fear. "You tried to kill me."

"No, I…"

She pushed him back, now a feeble baby. Her mind working through the possibilities. "You're going to get in to so much trouble. They're going to lock you up and throw away the key." She scrambled to her feet.

"It was an accident."

"A likely story."

"You shouldn't spread these lies," he told her desperately, taking her by the shoulders to shake some sense into her. Shaking and shaking. Her head banging repetitively against the wall. She looked ill, frightened, her acrylic fingernails scratching at his wrists, wanting to be free. He couldn't stop himself. His hands crept up to her neck like malignant spiders. Thumbs feeling the cartilage rough consistency of her windpipe. Testing and pressing it. Seeing how far it would go. She looked surprised now. Like a fish out of water.

When she stopped thrashing, he dropped her to the floor and staggered away. Oh god, he hadn't meant to do this. He really hadn't wanted to kill her.

Someone was laughing in the kitchen.

He ran through. The kitchen was empty. He hurried back into the living room, catching sight of the book, close to the body of his girlfriend. That book. He snatched it up, wanting to rip it apart. He wished he had never seen that poem. The poem. Those words. He opened up the book, flicking through the last pages, but the poem was no longer there. The biro pen writing remained but the words had changed.

'I did warn you.'

He started screaming. He screamed and screamed and screamed. He couldn't stop.

The police broke the door down when the screaming had stopped. The neighbours were terrified. A woman's body lay limp on the floor, her neck adorned with a choker of bruises. Pages from a paperback were scattered everywhere like feathers from a pillow fight. They found him in the hallway, his head on an angle looking at the world from an unbalanced viewpoint. Hanging from a noose made of braiding torn off the settee. Quite dead.

There was no note. No one was ever really sure why he did it. Obituaries were written. Polite mention was made of the book, but not too much fuss made: it had not been very good. Everyone praised the poem and mourned the fact that he would never be able to follow it up.

Somewhere his soul is still screaming.

My Nightmare

I am standing on the veranda. It is a cold spring day and my knuckles are freezing. They are bleached white as I grip the railing. I am screaming. Everything is still but the world is collapsing.

The last six years have not been easy. Looking back, I honestly do not know how I sometimes managed to continue. The fact that I still have a reasonable semblance of sanity ought to be something I should be proud of.

The money helped, it still does, - even though it was not quite as much as anyone expected we would get. No matter how idealistic we might like to be, money always helps. They say money doesn't matter. True, it doesn't make you happy. But it makes the road softer, in some cases even passable.

As soon as I was allowed, which wasn't soon enough for me, I left the city and moved up here to my mother. I had to get out of the city, away from the place where it had all gone so terribly wrong. I needed to be far away from people, culture, civilisation, and the media - the cursed media. They were one of the worst things. Not the worst, but it certainly felt as though they wanted to be.

My daughter is seven years old now. Her childhood has been so very different to how I imagined it would be when she was born. Despite it all, I think in some ways, it has been for the best. It's healthy here, you get the chance to be yourself. You can close your eyes and there is no noise. No rush of modern life. It is beautiful.

My mother lives in a cottage on the edge of a small village on the north Scottish coast. We're a long way from anywhere; only the hardcore hiking tourists ever appear. Which in some ways is surprising because the landscape is truly stunning, but then, the fact it is an empty wilderness is what makes it so stunning.

The small community is close knit. The speckled spread of cottages, crofts and farms are like a beating organism. Everyone knows everyone else. They all know what happened to me, but they don't talk about it - at least not to my face - and they don't judge me for it. In fact, I am sure they helped me more than I know in the beginning, by holding up a blockade of silence, pushing the unwelcome journalists away.

For the first two years we lived with my mother. She was a great help. I couldn't do very much at the start – I was a mental wreck – and she looked after my daughter as if she was her own. The locals helped my mother with chores, with keeping the unwanted visitors away. When winter started to approach, the Canadian from across the loch would come and chop wood. I was starting to come out of my catatonia by then. He was the first person, the first non-blood relative I started to really talk to.

Six years ago I was still married. His name was Leon and he was an artist. We both were, but after we became an item I took a step back. I was content with my small scale paintings. Leon was becoming a name in the art world. He was sensitive, easily offended and a deep thinker. Tall and musky, dark long hair; long, thin dexterous fingers. That deep, intense stare which just bore right through you. The first moment I saw him I was smitten. I would have done anything for that man.

It was a long flirtation – agonising at times for me – but we were eventually married four years after we had first met. We moved into an airy loft apartment. Leon liked to think of himself as alternative, but he wanted me married, bound to him. I was quite happy with the arrangement. I supported him in all he did. I was in love. I was so happy.

Ida was born almost a year after our wedding day. She was a wonderful, happy little baby, who could sleep through anything and rarely woke in the night. Perfect, when you consider what some mothers at the baby clinic said they suffered. She was great company for me when Leon was setting up an installation, engrossed in a painting or discussing art with friends. They had always been equally our friends before we were married, but as I settled into the role of wife and mother, I was pushed closer to the edge, more just an extension of Leon. I honestly didn't mind at the time.

When I started to regain my mind, come to terms with what had happened, my new friends coaxed me back into life. It was arranged that I would paint a large mural on one side of the village school. I started to learn Gaelic – a language which is still very alive in this part of Scotland. I went to the pub with locals of my own generation, attended the caelidhs and danced and tumbled until the sweat was pouring off my body as if I was in the shower.

Ida went to the primary school and quickly picked up the local language. I struggled more with it, but by then I was in my early thirties, and at such an age it is not so easy to pick up a new language. A completely new way of thinking.

Ida took her lessons at the school; I took mine with the Canadian. The Canadian who lived on the far side of the loch – something of enigma to me as much as I would have been to the local residences when I first moved in. As genuine as they were, with my background, anyone would have stopped and wondered.

The Canadian spoke fluent Gaelic, having learned it in Nova Scotia. The surprising fact is there are more Gaelic speakers in Canada than in Scotland. But he was something of a linguist anyway; speaking three obscure languages and English perfectly. He was a translator, working in solitude in the house that he had bought. Brought up in the great outdoors of Canada, he had then moved to mass population to study and work. He got a good reputation as a translator. Had interesting work he liked. He was still restless. At thirty he had emigrated and moved to Scotland, bought the house. People said it was a phase and wouldn't last. He'd been there for nine years by the time I moved to the village, and in many ways seemed on an equal footing with the long-standing residents of hundreds of generations.

People told me I picked up my Gaelic twang from him. I spoke Gaelic like a Canadian. Gregor, a local man born the same year as me, would always tease me about how I spoke when I tried to practise the language in the pub. It is still a standing good-natured subject of torment even today. Marie, his sister, always said not to mind him or the others. They were just jealous because I stuck out a little, was special. She said it was because Gregor secretly wanted me.

Whatever it was, it was good to be accepted. To be able to start again and feel that it was possible to move on from the past.

I am freezing cold. Shivering. The sound of my teeth chattering is echoing in the bathroom. I am thinking how glad I am that Ida is in school; that she is not witnessing this.

There is steam curling out from the shower cubicle. The bathroom door is closed and the room is warming up. He is unzipping my dress. The heavy, sodden fabric slips off my shoulders and slumps on the tiled floor. I am robotic. I cannot speak. He doesn't say anything. We don't need to talk. We now understand everything. Finally, after all these years, we know everything.

We are standing naked in the bathroom. He holds me close, his arms around my back. He kisses my neck and moves me into the shower. The hot water stings at my skin. It is good to begin to feel warm again. He is so close I could breathe him in.

I am calm.

That day. That day, that day. A split second decision and I might not have gone to the café. I could have gone to the park and fed the ducks with Ida. It would have been so different.

It was the café where our circle of friends spent most of their free time. Mostly artists, but there were a few musicians and writers in the group, as well as one rogue waiter that we never could quite place but fitted in perfectly well.

In the early afternoon I went to the café with Ida. I was missing Leon. The group was quite amicable to having a child within their midst during the day – especially Leon's child – and Ida would fall asleep despite the chatter. Bickering, the occasional knocked wine glass and she was oblivious to it all.

Leon was stood at the bar with three other painters. They were talking avidly. Leon didn't see me until Mattias, a short Swede studying art in London, turned and saw me, calling out my name. Leon caught my eye and smiled. Ida wiggled on my hip. I walked up to him and he kissed my forehead. I nestled in to his chest. The top three buttons of his shirt were unfastened and a few twists of chest hair were showing. I could smell his scent, feel his heat. Just wanted to melt there. Leon gave me a brief hug and tickled Ida's nose.

"Darling, Fleah's in the back room, why don't you go and see her?"

"Oh."

Leon looked tired. "We're just in the middle of something."

Mattias laughed. "Big argument about art."

"Discussion," Ronny corrected.

One of those conversations. Leon could get so involved, so wound up. His hand gave a slight shake. He was incredibly passionate about art. I loved art, I worked as a painter, I loved beauty, but I had never really understood his engorging intensity. It seemed a bit much sometimes, but that was his way.

I forced a bright smile. "I'll go out back and see Fleah, then. Come soon."

Fleah was a small, butch-looking woman with long dreadlocks and a face like uncooked pastry. She made her living from street busking, either on the violin or mandolin, and had a surprisingly far-reaching reputation on the street across the south of England. If you didn't know her, you would give her one glance and be sure she was thinking about biting your ankles off. In truth, she was incredibly kind and soft hearted.

For the next hour or so I sat with Fleah at the back table by the window in the adjacent room to the bar. There was a lush window seat running across the back of the room, where we sat. A lot of the party had left their jackets here, and Ida gathered the coats together to build a den under the window seat before promptly falling asleep. One of the artists joined us at the table to talk. The café owner came in to take a spare table cloth out of the small storage cupboard. Finishing his chores, he left the rest of the work to his assistant and joined us at the table for a glass of wine.

Everything stopped when we heard the first shot. It had come from the front of the café. Conversation faltered; we looked uncertainly at one another. David, the café owner, stood up as if to investigate the situation. He was about to say something when another two shots broke the uneasy silence. His assistant started screaming.

David ran to the front of the café. Fleah stood up and picked up the empty wine bottle aggressively. The other man – to my shame I don't remember his name – cautiously approached the archway to the bar. I was on my knees now gathering up Ida, still mashed into the jumble of coats, to me.

The shots started to grow more furious, like tapping out a jazz beat. There was screaming – so terrified it was base, animal, you couldn't tell whether it was man or woman. The artist at the archway staggered back as Mattias rushed into the room. His shirt was covered in sticky thick blood. He looked like a corpse, only his hoarse, ragged breathing could convince you otherwise. He saw me clutching Ida and ran at us.

"He told me to get you hidden," he garbled, weakly pulling me up. He drew open the storage cupboard door and pushed me into the tight space. I saw Fleah moving towards the archway. She'd smashed the bottle open on the side of the table, as if that was going to save her.

The door shut in my face and we were pitched into darkness. The shelves dug into my back. I crumpled on the floor, shoved in the corner, and held Ida to me, praying to God she wouldn't wake up to all of this. Praying to God that she wouldn't wake up and start screaming.

The shouting came closer and I heard Fleah call out something. Shouting. Screaming. More shots. Something heavy thumped against the door and slipped down against the surface. I squeezed my eyes shut and tried to think of something else. I didn't want to be here, in this situation.

One final shot and the silence abruptly returned. One steady set of footsteps moved deeper into the room. I heard a man somewhere swear and say that they had to get out of here. There were no survivors.

I don't know how long it was before I dared to move. I slid my hand up in the dark until I felt the door handle. My fingers were shaking. I gently pushed at the door but it wouldn't move.

"Mummy?" Her tired, barely-awake voice came from somewhere in the bundle I was clinging onto.

"Go back to sleep," I whispered to her.

I gave the door a harder push and a slit of light broke through into the cupboard. A couple of kicks and it was open enough for me to slip through.

Mattias had been valiantly blocking our way, slumped across the door with a bullet in his head. There was blood everywhere. It was surreal to find myself in this butchery. I must have been in shock, because I moved quite calmly through that back room, passing by the corpse of Fleah, the bullet-ridden body of the artist, slumped against the side of the archway, thick smears pasted down the wall.

My footsteps were painfully loud as I stepped on the broken glass in the bar. I homed in on Leon, lying on his back, his chest full of bullet holes, splashes of other people's blood across his face. The breath caught in my throat. The bile built up in my stomach. Leon opened his eyes and saw me. I thought I was going to be sick.

"Leon."

I have never seen agony of the like I saw on his face. "I've changed my mind," he coughed. "I'm sorry."

And right there in front of me, he died.

I didn't smile for a long time. There were occasions when I doubted I would see the year out. That I would be sane the following week. I did eventually have a breakdown, but the first few weeks were a blur. Caught up in shock, still unable to comprehend that everyone I knew in London was dead. That my beloved, my Leon was gone.

Of course, this was like gold for the media. The newspapers were full of nothing else. Reporters camped outside our family home, wanting the inside secrets, the bloody details from me. I started to clam up. I quit keeping up with the news.

The police had their questions. At one time I think I was a suspect. I know I was, although they would not tell me. All the surviving relatives were to one degree or another. A dead artist's work is so much more valuable than when he was alive, especially with all this media coverage. And as Leon was the highest ranking artist of the victims, I was naturally the highest ranking suspect.

I don't think anyone ever thought I had gone on a killing spree, rather that I was somehow involved with the shooters who had arrived and committed the massacre. I have no idea who they were. The fact is, no one does. To this day no one actually knows why it happened. The police think they caught one of the men responsible, but he was killed in gang warfare soon afterwards, and the official police line was that he had never told them anything of use.

I was the only surviving witness and I saw nothing. The only one who could have brought some justice for Leon and I failed. I fell apart.

By the time I moved up to my mother's, the police had given up investigating me, admitting that I was not involved. I was a wreck at this point, barely speaking, completely incapable. When the police were not insinuating, the media were screaming, flashing cameras in my face, making millions out of what had happened.

I gradually got better, learned to trust people, if only a select few. I still wear my scars, but I did manage to start living again. I remember the first time I smiled after that day. When I felt as though I would be able to offer Ida a good kind of childhood. That we still did have a promising future.

I had fallen into the habit of going to the local pub frequently on an evening. I didn't drink, but in these isolated communities, such places are a point for human connection. Not all people are bad. There were often music nights; just locals getting together informally to play. The Canadian was fond of the guitar, and would write his own songs to sing – with his own particular brand of humour, very down-to-earth and dry. He had a deep throaty voice. A couple of women did clog dancing, which made quite a rustic bass line. With the other local musicians, they formed an impressive impromptu little band.

Some of them would play in the village hall when it was caelidh time and the rest of us would go dancing and drinking. The lights would be like candlelight, the temperature in the building rising as people danced, the sweat pouring. It was at one of these occasions, towards the end of a fast dance you were sure you had become airborne, that he kissed me. It wasn't love like with Leon. It hadn't hit me in the first moment, but had gradually built without me realising. I couldn't imagine ever being without him now.

It was another year before we moved in with the Canadian, with Anthony. I hadn't wanted to rush anything, not after what had happened, not after I had become a widow. I was worried about Ida, as well as my mother, but the only person who ever seemed to show any doubts about the relationship was me.

And you might have thought that was enough for any one body to bear. More than a fair share of tragedy. Life doesn't work like that.

Six years later and I am walking back up the track through the trees to our home. I have just taken Ida to school. Anthony has driven out to the next village, larger, where they have a post office, to pick up a parcel. I am alone.

There is a man sitting on the veranda of our home. The front door is not locked, but he wouldn't know that. He obviously doesn't come from here. He expects everything to be nailed down. His expensive car is parked by the shed. He has probably locked it and set the alarm. I don't know who he is or why he is here.

He stands up when he sees me approach. I see he has a newspaper in his hands. I haven't read one since that day. He calls my name like a question, but I can see he already knows who I am. We have never met but he knows who I am because he is a journalist. I have learned to see their kind.

I silently walk towards him and stop at the veranda steps. "What do you want?"

"Have you seen this?" He opens the paper and pushes it towards me. Without thinking I take it, seeing pages and pages of feature articles, colour photographs. Leon's work. Our wedding photograph. Headlines and names. I catch sight of words. 'Police evidence recently released to the public explains…' I crumple the paper up and throw it at him.

"Get out of here."

"I'd just like a quote. A few of your thoughts. You must have some reaction to this kind of news."

I push past him and march into the building.

"Or did you know about it before?" he shouts after me.

I take the shot gun out of the gun cupboard. I never thought I would be able to handle one of these, but I am so furious. I load it quickly as I am walking to the door.

"Get off my property."

He sees the shotgun, looks surprised and walks slowly down from the veranda. He is probably surprised to see me of all people handling a gun. He looks like he is about to make some smart comment about me being involved. Everyone knows I was not involved.

"I have nothing to say to you. Get off my property."

"I would just like a comment from you on what the police have released."

I aim and surprise myself by shattering his back window in the car. Beginner's luck that I hit my target with my first ever shot. He holds up his hands, looking really scared now. He is probably beginning to realise how serious this is, that it actually happened and the survivors were devastated by it. It's not just some nasty story to read about in the newspapers, pick apart during the coffee break at work. This is life.

Stumbling, he falls into the car. The engine starts and the vehicle speeds away. I drop the shotgun onto the veranda. I don't feel well. And then I see the crumpled newspaper lying on the ground.

There is screaming inside my head. It is on the outside. It is me. I don't know where to begin or what to do. I want to stop. I can't cope. It was all my fault.

I run away from the house, down to the loch. I can't stop. My feet enter the icy water and I lunge into the loch, gasping with the sharp pain of the cold water. I want to be numb. I want to stop.

Words and lines flash at me. Quotes from the police. From other family members who didn't have to be there. Didn't have to see the blood. Witness the carnage. Hear his last words. Spend six years wondering what they meant and never really solving the puzzle until now.

The three men who had gone into the café and systematically executed the people inside were not opportunistic thieves. They were not mad men and they were not there for revenge. They had a time and a place in their diaries and money in their back pocket. A lot more in the bank. They were paid assassins, hit men, executioners. They were to exterminate everyone and anyone who happened to be in the café, although there was only one target. One man they were paid to kill. Leon.

Perhaps we had always known this was planned. Leon had been making the headlines in the last couple of years. He was becoming a well known name. He had been producing some controversial work. And the fact that a whole café of artists had been massacred suggested planning and intent.

That wasn't enough to send me to the loch. It was when I read what the police had known, the thing we would not have guessed, that I fell apart. It was Leon who had hired those men. He wanted to die, but he didn't have the courage to do it himself. Or maybe he wanted to make some kind of a statement. Either way, he was suffering from depression and he wanted to die. He wanted to die so badly.

The water is soaking up the skirts of my dress. I think of the happy home. Of our new baby, of me, the happy wife. Of my husband. My husband who didn't tell me that he wished he was dead. I didn't make him miserable. I made him want to die.

I was the one who walked out of the carnage but I should have died there. I am still alive, still connecting with other people. I wonder how long it will be before Anthony wants to end it all.

I have the newspaper in my hands. I am crying. It's hard to breathe properly. I rip the pages out, throw them into the loch. How can this be true? How could he do this to me? What did I do to him? He has become a stranger.

I can't see properly. My vision blurred. I just want to sink below the surface. Make this all stop. I throw the last of the paper to the water. Hear something. Twist and look back. A figure is running to the shore. Maybe there is a still a chance.

Lovers of Old Films
Ophelia Finsen

Fresh from university and eager for the rest of his life, Edward Gable moves to York to start a position in a graduate training scheme. And whilst real life may not meet his expectations, the building he moves into can more than compensate for the lack of excitement. Certainly everyone is friendly and helpful, but there are secrets no one wants to talk about – and if you find yourself living in a building with Sophia Loren, you know something out of the ordinary is going to happen.

Ever wanted to be your idol?
You might want to think again…

www.ingramcontent.com/pod-product-compliance
Lightning Source LLC
Chambersburg PA
CBHW031847170626
46807CB00004B/1657